Puddin, Pirates,
and the
Problem with Power

BRAVE BOOKS

DOM-A-TRON

THE OLD ISLANDS

Doomsdome

Burrycanter

UTOPIA

Freedom Island

WIGGAMORE WOOD

Rushington

SUMA SAVANNA

Hive Have

Furenzy Park

Toke-A-Toke

Wonder Well

Capitol

RAKA RAIN FOREST

Mushroom Village

Deserted Desert

Mt. Avalerif

Sky Tree

Snapfast Meadow

CAR-A-LAGO COAST

Starlotte City

Gray Landing

Home of the Brave

Welcome to Freedom Island, Home of the Brave, where good battles evil and truth prevails. Defend Freedom's Law by completing the BRAVE Challenge at the back of the book.

Watch this video for an introduction to the story and BRAVE Universe!

Saga Two: Iron Chaos

Book 1

Puddin, Pirates, and the Problem with Power

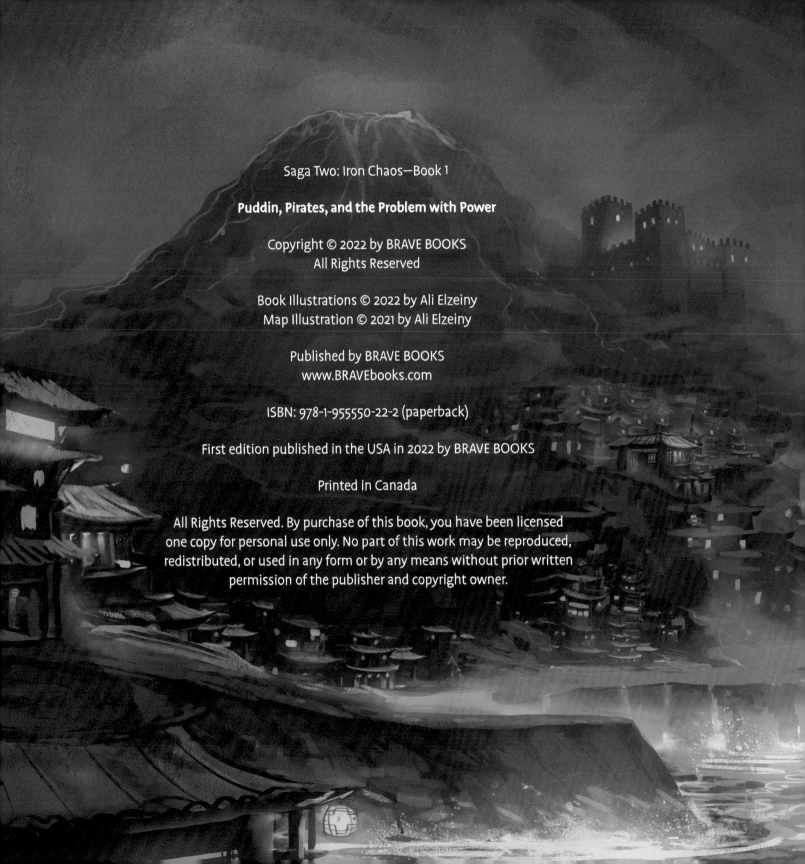

Saga Two: Iron Chaos—Book 1

Puddin, Pirates, and the Problem with Power

Book Illustrations © 2022 by Ali Elzeiny
Map Illustration © 2021 by Ali Elzeiny

Published by BRAVE BOOKS
www.BRAVEbooks.com

ISBN: 978-1-955550-22-2 (paperback)

First edition published in the USA in 2022 by BRAVE BOOKS

Printed in Canada

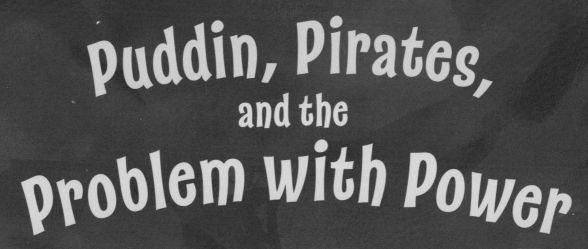

Puddin, Pirates, and the Problem with Power

BRAVE BOOKS and **Robby Starbuck**

Art by **Ali Elzeiny**

I am Puddin, the stealthiest, most feared female warrior of the Lava Tribe.

I just completed my most dangerous mission yet: stealing Freedom's Law.

My tribe hated Freedom's Law because it had too many rules. So I teamed up with the pirates to rewrite the Law. We would only make one rule:

NOBODY CAN TELL US WHAT TO DO.

Thanks to my new pirate friends and my incredible sneakery, I was able to race home to Mt. Avalerif with the Law in my paws.

When I reached Mt. Avalerif, Robby hooted at me: "You shouldn't have stolen the Law, Puddin. Hoot! Hoot! Freedom's Law lets you speak freely and use your staff to defend yourself. It protects us by making sure no one takes too much power. Hoot! If you're smart, you'll put the Law back where it belongs."

"No," I said. "The pirate captain, Lester, will melt the Law in the volcano and rewrite it. Imagine how much fun we'll have once it says whatever we want!"

Robby shook his head, and I turned away to give the Law to Lester.

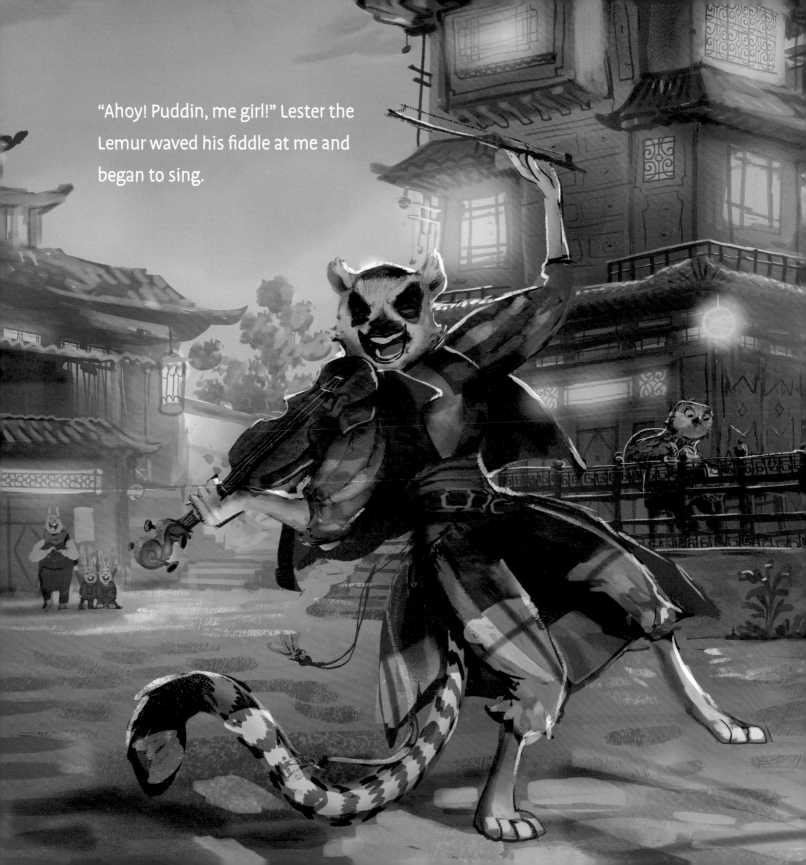

"Ahoy! Puddin, me girl!" Lester the Lemur waved his fiddle at me and began to sing.

"Yer stealing the Law was flawless,
And soon the whole land'll be lawless!
When we melt this law down in the burning hot fire,
The new "Lester Law" will grant all we desire!"

But before we could take the law up the mountain, a clear voice
boomed across the town. "Stop, you destroyers of freedom!"

"Hoot! It's Team BRAVE!"
Robby's eyes grew wide.

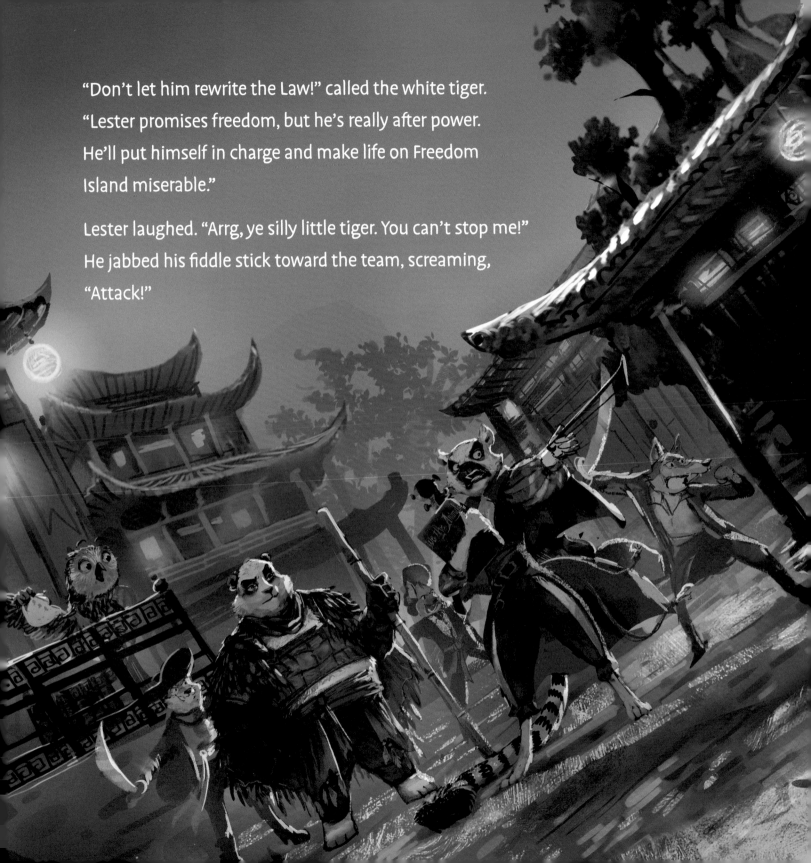

"Don't let him rewrite the Law!" called the white tiger. "Lester promises freedom, but he's really after power. He'll put himself in charge and make life on Freedom Island miserable."

Lester laughed. "Arrg, ye silly little tiger. You can't stop me!" He jabbed his fiddle stick toward the team, screaming, "Attack!"

All around me, I heard clinking, clashing, and whips lashing!

A net whooshed past my head, and Lester let loose a tangled, strangled, "Yo ho—oh no!"

Team BRAVE lept from the rooftops, readied their weapons, and grabbed the Law from the pirate captian.

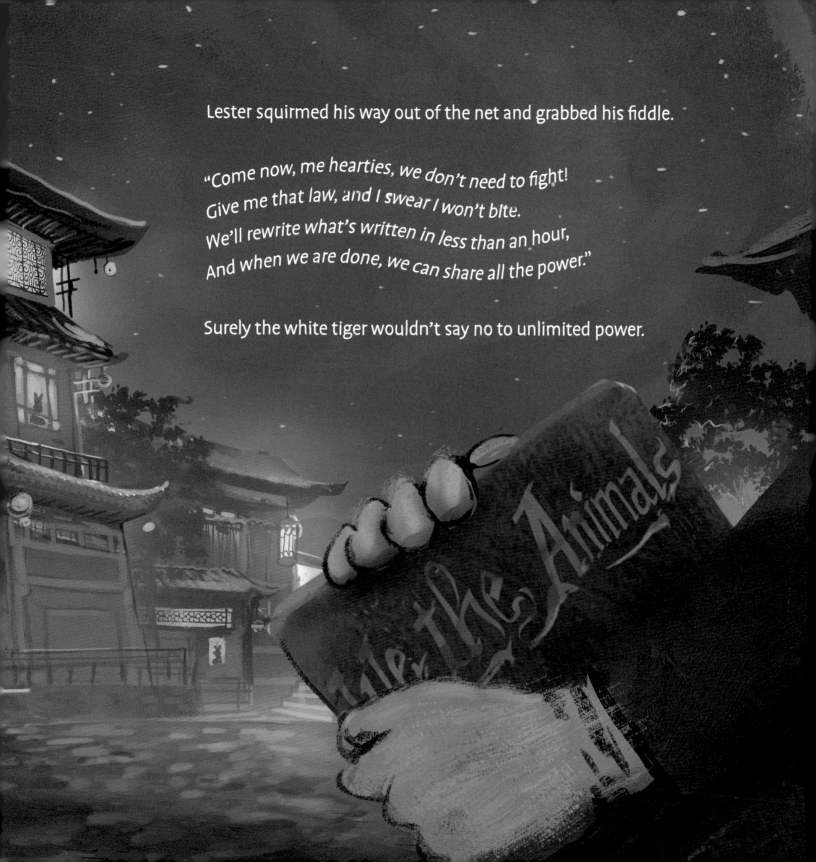

Lester squirmed his way out of the net and grabbed his fiddle.

"Come now, me hearties, we don't need to fight!
Give me that law, and I swear I won't bite.
We'll rewrite what's written in less than an hour,
And when we are done, we can share all the power."

Surely the white tiger wouldn't say no to unlimited power.

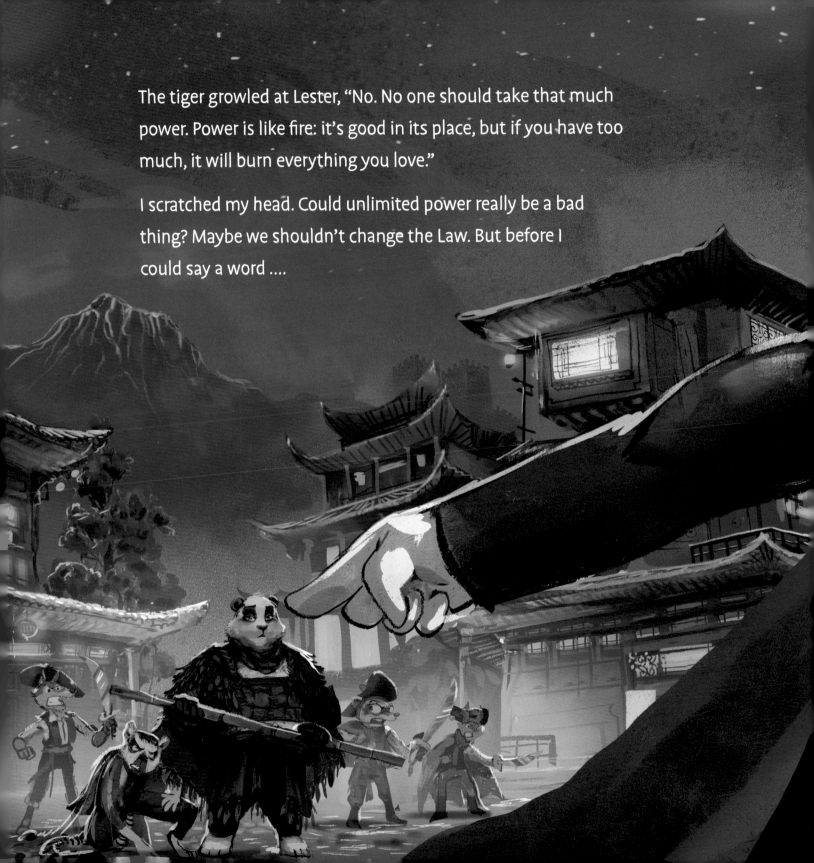

The tiger growled at Lester, "No. No one should take that much power. Power is like fire: it's good in its place, but if you have too much, it will burn everything you love."

I scratched my head. Could unlimited power really be a bad thing? Maybe we shouldn't change the Law. But before I could say a word ....

"Pirates, NOW!" Lester screeched. From the volcanic lake, his newly improved, lava-proof pirate ship sent flaming cannonballs into our town.

I watched, helpless.

IRON CHAOS

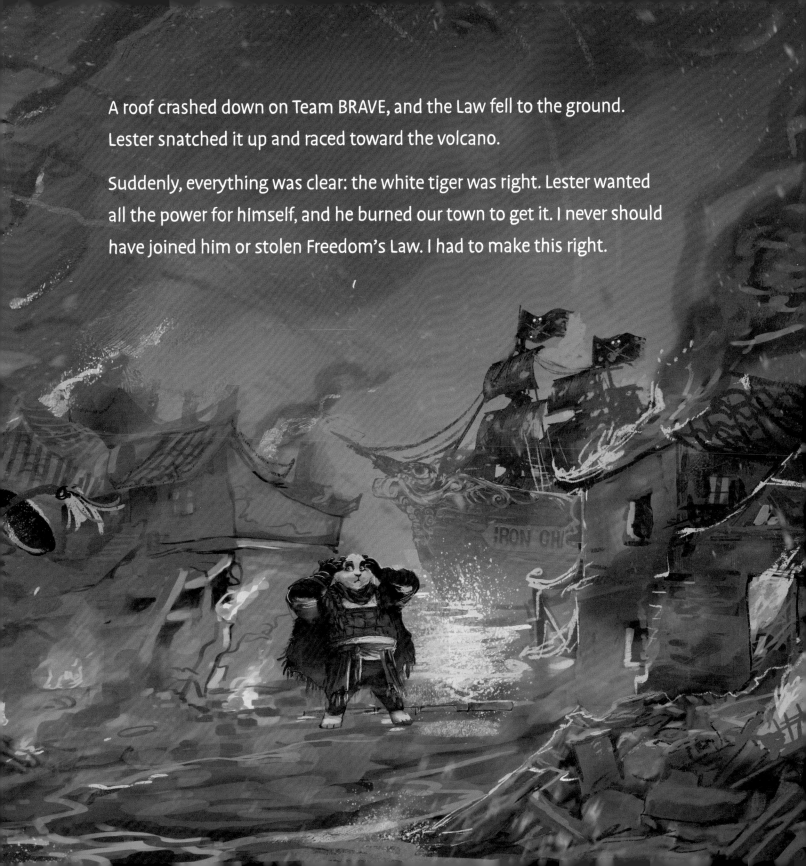

A roof crashed down on Team BRAVE, and the Law fell to the ground. Lester snatched it up and raced toward the volcano.

Suddenly, everything was clear: the white tiger was right. Lester wanted all the power for hImself, and he burned our town to get it. I never should have joined him or stolen Freedom's Law. I had to make this right.

I rushed to rescue Team BRAVE from the fallen roof, straining and struggling under its great weight. Together, we ran up the volcano after Lester.

As Lester reached the top, the gorilla shot his coconut cannon.

"Ouchy, my fiddle!" Lester yelped. Freedom's Law sprang from his paws and bounced once—twice—

My heart stopped.

Freedom's Law disappeared into the volcano.

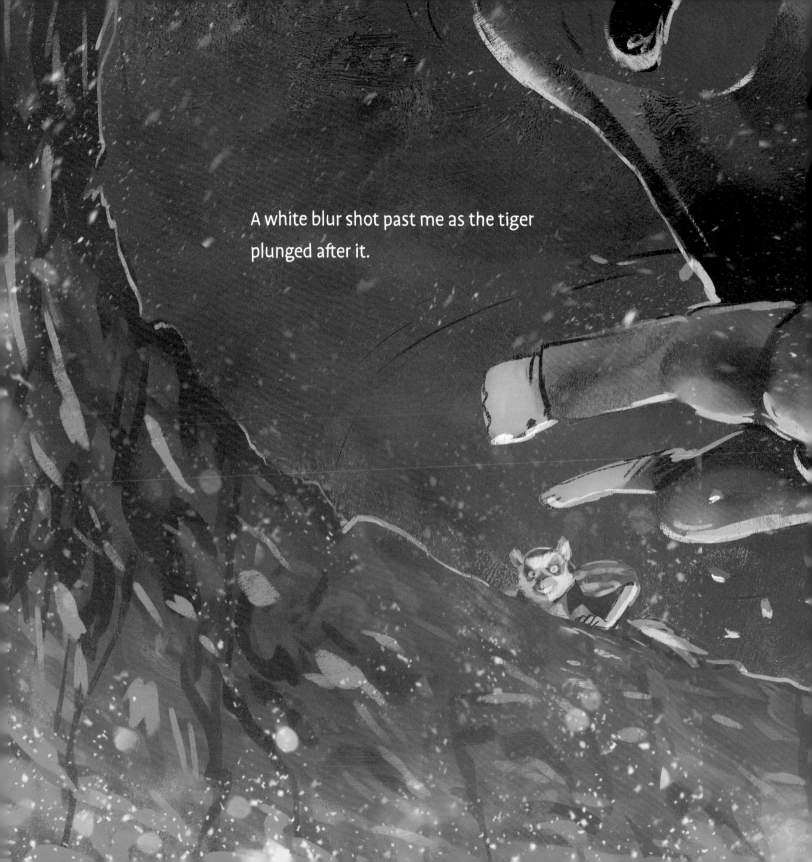

A white blur shot past me as the tiger plunged after it.

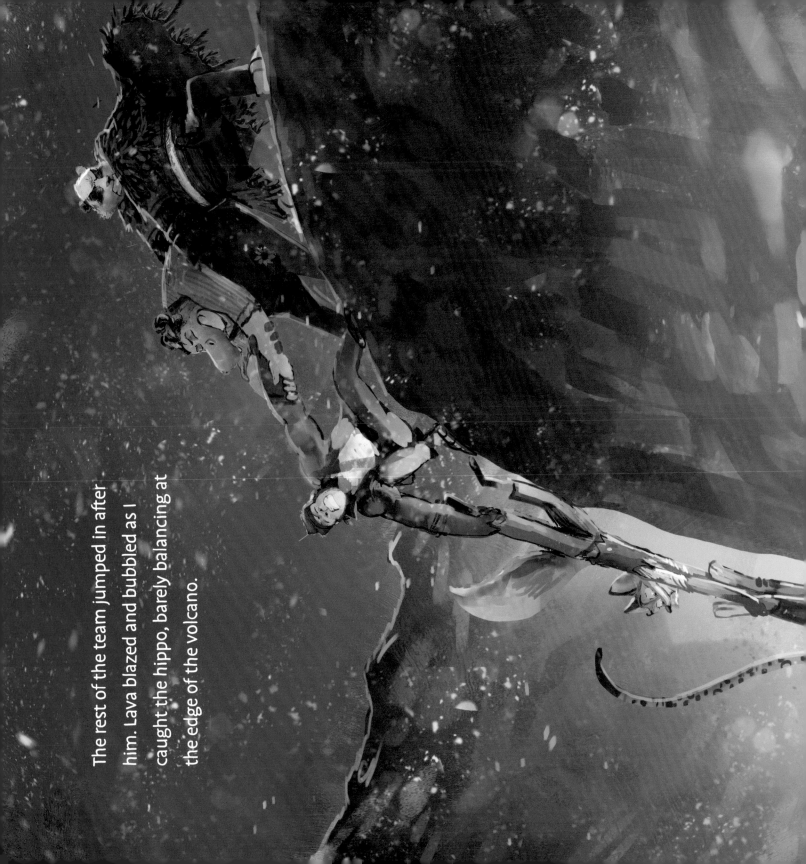

The rest of the team jumped in after him. Lava blazed and bubbled as I caught the hippo, barely balancing at the edge of the volcano.

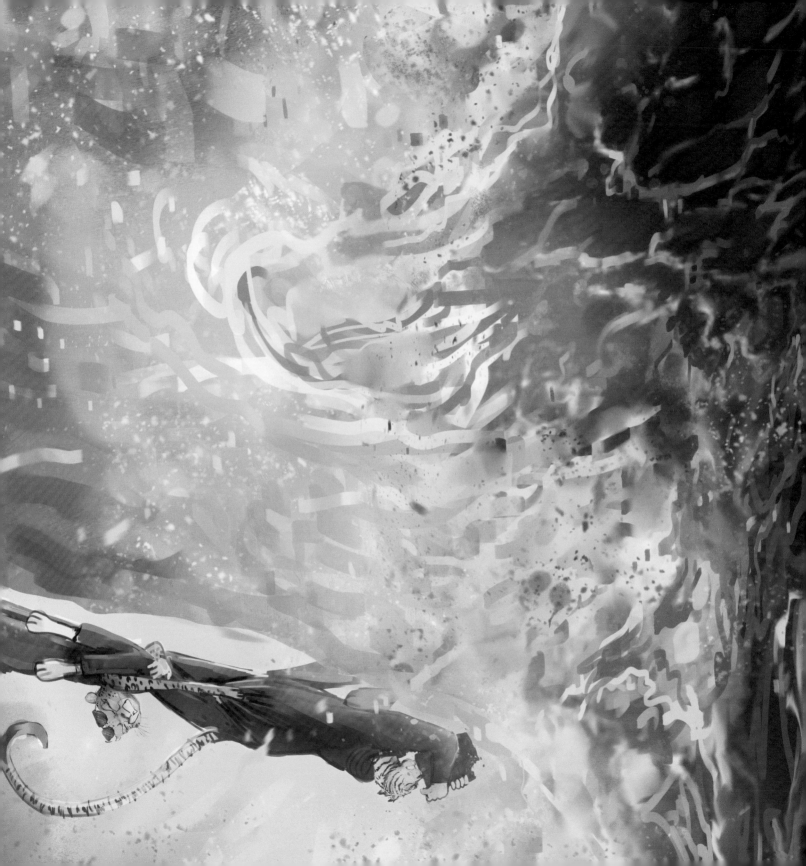

With my help, the team climbed out. Freedom's Law was safe once more.
Lester and his pirates sailed away, grumbling that they'd be back soon.

I shook paws with Team BRAVE, who told me their names were

Bongo **R**ebel **A**sher **V**alor **E**va

Together, we returned Freedom's Law to its rightful place.

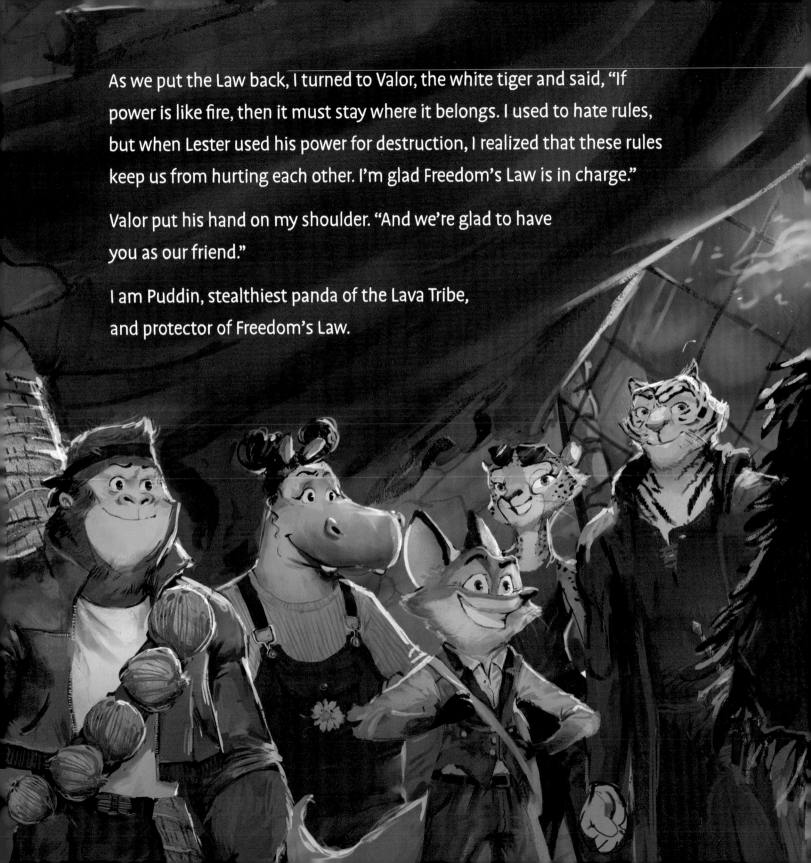

As we put the Law back, I turned to Valor, the white tiger and said, "If power is like fire, then it must stay where it belongs. I used to hate rules, but when Lester used his power for destruction, I realized that these rules keep us from hurting each other. I'm glad Freedom's Law is in charge."

Valor put his hand on my shoulder. "And we're glad to have you as our friend."

I am Puddin, stealthiest panda of the Lava Tribe, and protector of Freedom's Law.

YOUR MISSION

BRAVE Cadets,

Lester and his sneaky pirates have
their eyes on Freedom's Law. If we're
not careful, he might snatch it again.
Complete the two missions below to save
the day:

- Prepare for battle by updating your
  map with the Puddin and flag stickers
  included.

- Defeat the evil pirates in the BRAVE
  Challenge, and celebrate your victory
  with an epic reward.

- As a bonus, can you find all nine times
  Robby the Owl shows up in the story?

Team BRAVE is counting on your help. Are
you ready to be BRAVE?

INTRODUCING...
ROBBY STARBUCK

Robby Starbuck is a husband, father, and film director who is dedicated to America. Ever since his family fled Marxist Cuba, Robby has been passionate about equipping others to chase the American Dream. After being canceled for his conservative values, Robby and his wife, Landon, moved their family from Calabasas, California to central Tennessee, where Robby is now running for Congress. Through this BRAVE book and the BRAVE Challenge, he's helping families across America reclaim their passion for our nation and our Constitution.

ROBBY SUGGESTS:

"Welcome to the BRAVE Challenge! I am so excited that I was able to help kick-start Saga 2 of BRAVE Books, and I hope that you and your family enjoy the games and discussions."

Constitution: A document written by and with the consent of the people to function as the highest law of the land. It limits the power of the nation's governing powers.

INTRODUCTION

Welcome BRAVE Cadets! The BRAVE Challenge is a quick and fun way to drive home key lessons illustrated in the story. Your mission for this BRAVE Challenge is to defend Freedom's Law from the pirates.

ADDITIONAL VIDEO CONTENT

For a fun addition to the BRAVE Challenge experience, scan Iggy Guana's QR code or search for BRAVE Books on YouTube. In the videos linked there, Super Secret Special Agent J explains more about the topic in a way that the whole family will enjoy.

HOW TO PLAY

To get started, grab a sheet of paper and a pencil, and draw a scoreboard like the one shown. In the end, if the BRAVE Cadets (kids) can put more points on this scoreboard than the pirates, they have won the challenge and saved Freedom's Law. Before starting Game One, choose a prize for winning. For example ...

- Family game night
- Riding bikes
- Baking cupcakes or cookies
- Whatever gets your kiddos excited!

BRAVE Cadets	Pirates
ⅧⅡ	Ⅲ

GAME #1 - AVOID-N-CAPTURE

LESSON

Like games, a society can't function effectively with either too few or too many rules.

OBJECTIVE

Welcome to Mt. Avalerif! You must prove to the pirates that too many or too few rules will result in chaos. Do this by playing three rounds of Avoid-n-Capture (Hide and Seek) with a different number of rules each round.

MATERIALS

A timer.

INSTRUCTIONS

ROUND 1

1. The BRAVE Cadets will hide, and the pirates (parents) must find them.

2. The pirates will have complete control over the rules during the first round. At any point, they can call out rules like:

   a. The pirates may keep their eyes open while the BRAVE Cadets are hiding.
   b. The BRAVE Cadets must hop on one leg when looking for a spot to hide.
   c. The BRAVE Cadets must begin singing.
   d. The BRAVE Cadets must respond to their name being called.
   e. Or anything else.

ROUND 2

3. For this round, there are no rules for either team. This means:

   a. The pirates can begin searching whenever they want.
   b. The BRAVE Cadets can hide however they want.
   c. The BRAVE Cadets can remain uncaptured even if the pirates finds them.
   d. And much more.

ROUND 3

4. The last round follows the regular rules of Hide and Seek.

5. The pirates close their eyes for 30 seconds while the BRAVE Cadets hide.

TIMER

Each round lasts one minute.

SCORING

Round 1: The pirates get one point for every cadet caught and BRAVE Cadets get one point for each remaining cadet.

Round 2: At the end of the round, no points are awarded to either team.

Round 3: Same as Round 1.

TALK ABOUT IT

1. In the game, did you prefer it when the pirates made up all the rules? Why or why not?

2. In the game, round two had no rules. How does having absolutely no rules make it hard to play the game?

3. In the book, Team BRAVE fought for freedom by defending Freedom's Law from the pirates. Is Freedom Island a better place to live in if there are rules or not? Why?

4. Think of another game (football, baseball, tag), and explain how the game would or wouldn't work if there were no rules.

5. In the game, the last round had a fair amount of rules. Did the game work better this way? Why or why not? Why is it important to have the right amount of rules in a game?

6. If society is like a game, what would happen in our country if there weren't any rules or laws? Why is it important to have the right rules in our country?

ROBBY SUGGESTS

"The Founding Fathers intentionally built a system of rules to guide America. These rules help to uphold our freedom as long as we function inside them. However, when leaders make rules that take away our freedom, society can't function, and that's what the next game is about.

GAME #2 - TIC-TAC-TOO MUCH POWER

LESSON

Too much power brings tyranny.

OBJECTIVE

The pirates want to change all the rules and take all the power. The BRAVE Cadets must show the pirates why too much power is a bad thing while playing different rounds of tic-tac-toe.

MATERIALS

One ball, a pencil, and a sheet of paper.

INSTRUCTIONS

1. The pirates will take turns playing tic-tac-toe with BRAVE Cadets.

2. During the first round, the pirates will hold the ball of power.

3. The ball lets you change any rule you want. You can take two turns in a row, you can turn X's into O's, or anything else you like!

4. For the second round, give the ball of power to a BRAVE Cadet.

5. Repeat the game until everyone has played while holding the ball of power.

SCORING

At the end of the game, give both teams 6 points for this game.

TALK ABOUT IT

1. In the game, did the team holding the ball make rules that were good for both teams or just themselves? Why or why not?

2. Did you enjoy this version better than regular tic-tac-toe?

3. If the power was split between both players, do you think the game would have been more fair?

4. In the story, the pirates wanted to have complete control over all of Freedom Island. Would Freedom Island be better off only having one ruler who only cared about themselves?

ROBBY SUGGESTS

"When the person in charge makes a rule that only helps himself, he takes away the people's freedom. This is why our ability to choose our leaders as American citizens is such an important responsibility."

5. In the story, Valor refused unlimited power. Why do you think he did that? Can having too much power hurt those you love?

> *"They promise them freedom, while they themselves are slaves of depravity—for 'people are slaves to whatever has mastered them.'"*
>
> **2 Peter 2:19** (NIV)

6. If you were the one in complete control over everyone else, would that make everyone else happy? How would you feel if someone else had complete control over you?

7. With all the rules in America, do you think it would be better if many people helped make the rules or just one person?

GAME #3 - RULES OF THE LAND

LESSON
A good constitution protects the rights of the people.

OBJECTIVE
The pirates want to know how a Constitution and rules would protect them. BRAVE Cadets, show them that when the Constitution and rules they put in place are upheld, it protects and helps the entire tribe.

MATERIALS
Sticky notes or ripped pieces of paper and a pencil.

INSTRUCTIONS

1. Provide a stack of sticky notes for each BRAVE Cadet.

2. Each BRAVE Cadet will try to claim the most territory by placing sticky notes on furniture and items around the house.

3. Designate a location as the base for storing everyone's sticky notes. BRAVE Cadets must keep all their unused notes in a stack at this location and may only hold one of their own notes at a time.

4. They must write their name or initials on the sticky note before leaving to place it on items. Leave the writing utensil next to the stack of unused sticky notes.

5. Each piece of furniture or item can only have one sticky note at a time.

6. Designate another location as a prison.

7. The BRAVE Cadets can choose to remove another cadet's sticky note, hide it, and replace it with their own. However, if a parent catches the cadet stealing a note, the cadet must go to prison for 20 seconds.

SCORING

At the end of the game, each BRAVE Cadet will only get points for how many of their papers are placed on pieces of furniture, NOT for any notes that they stole.

Take the highest team member's score and assign it to the whole team.

Read after the game: The pirates will get one point (up to 6 points) for every sticky note stolen.

ONE CHILD MODIFICATION

Have a parent place sticky notes around the room and also police stealing.

TIMER

The game lasts two minutes (parents, adjust as needed).

TALK ABOUT IT

1. At the end of the game, you were only awarded points for the sticky notes you had on the furniture. Did stealing help you win? If you played again, would you steal next time?

ROBBY SUGGESTS

"Good laws protect people's lives and rights by punishing people who take those away. Because people know that stealing leads to punishment, they're more likely to choose not to steal. This is better for everyone."

2. In the game, there were certain laws put in place in order to stop the stealing of other people's sticky notes. Do you think it's a good thing to have those laws? What would happen if there weren't any?

3. Did you like it when people stole from you? Why or why not? Would you like it if there was no one to help protect you and your belongings? Why or why not?

"Anyone who has been stealing must steal no longer, but must work, doing something useful with their own hands, that they may have something to share with those in need."

Ephesians 4:28 (NIV)

4. In the story, Puddin saw how Team BRAVE fought to protect Freedom's Law. How did watching them fight for freedom help her realize that laws need to be protected?

5. Go back and read the definition of the Constitution on page 43. How does a good Constitution lead to good rule-making? If the Constitution had been written by people focused on their own power, what kind of laws would we have in America?

6. What do you think would happen if people made laws with other people's needs in mind?

TALLY ALL THE POINTS TO SEE WHO WON!

FINAL THOUGHTS FROM ROBBY

In the story, Freedom's Law protected the animals of Freedom Island from harsh rules that would take away their freedom. It promised that the animals of Freedom Island could make their own choices, as long as those choices didn't take away the freedom of another animal. In real life, the U. S. Constitution does the same thing for Americans. Some people, like Lester, want to take all the power for themselves by getting rid of the Constitution as we know it. Just like Team BRAVE fought for Freedom's Law, it's our responsibility to fight for the Constitution of the United States.

Make sure to visit

Hive Haven

In Saga Two: Book 2

WELCOME TO

HIVE HAVEN